The Drone Outside

Kristine Ong Muslim

The Drone Outside
by Kristine Ong Muslim

ISBN: 978-1-908125-54-5

Cover Art by David Rix

Publication Date: December 2017

All text copyright 2017 Kristine Ong Muslim

Acknowledgments

Grateful acknowledgement is made to the editors of the following publications in which the early versions of these stories first appeared or are forthcoming: *Liminoid Magazine* (edited by Marie Schutt and Brenton Woodward), *Outlook Springs* (edited by Jeremy John Parker), *Marked to Die: A Tribute to Mark Samuels* (Snuggly Books, 2016; edited by Justin Isis), *Fiction Southeast* (edited by Chris Tusa), and *Sunvault: Stories of Solarpunk & Eco-Speculation* (Upper Rubber Boot Books, 2017; edited by Phoebe Wagner and Brontë Wieland).

Contents

Kilroy Was Here

On the sixth day of June, we stormed 108 Tower at 9 Elone Street to unplug the machine. We came to unhook the wires—both invisible and not—that tethered the machine to us and to our lives.

Once again it was Virgil who brought much-needed light to guide our passage. He found and held down the invisible lever of the invisible switch on the wall of the temperature-controlled cleanroom where the machine, long believed to be immortal and indestructible, was housed. Keeping the machine from overheating, the cleanroom's subzero environment was a welcome respite from the heatwave enveloping the city.

We got busy, starting with the compressors and the mufflers lining the underside of the prefab chamber that shielded the machine from long-wave interference. We followed the shut-down sequence to a tee, performed the synchronized movements rehearsed multiple times before—red crossed with yellow, blue depressed with white, countermand tab, suppressor toggle switch flipped down, and then the code: K1LR0Y_W@$_HERE

It did not take long for the floor to be blanketed with a tangle of color-coded wires and translucent jacks—all mute with desperate pleas of *look, look at the remains of your beautiful life. There's still time. Plug back in, plug back in, plug back in. Don't let the machine die because you will die with it.* One of us, someone from the tribe of susceptibles, looked longingly at the bloodless sprawl, as if something inside him had indeed died with the machine. He knew better than that but a lifetime of conditioning had a way of asserting itself, of making him feel that with the machine's death, something had, indeed, been taken from him. We let him be. We allowed him to savor his grief.

Somebody was quick to point out a dent and a couple of faint scratches on one of the three simulated doors—painful reminders of last year's suicides and failed attempt to unplug the machine.

Our exit from the building was uneventful—as expected. The planned escape route involved Virgil willingly giving up his hand to continue holding down the invisible lever of the invisible switch on the wall of one of the narrow passageways. This was the one lever that chomped down with a mouthful of blades. There was no getting around its main requirement of sacrifice. So, with enough light to go on, we crossed the barrier, paused for a moment to wait for Virgil so we could quickly slap and wind a tourniquet around the bleeding stump of his severed left arm. Local anesthetics and a torch for cauterization awaited him inside our parked vehicle. He would mend in time.

When we made our way out of 108 Tower at 9 Elone Street that sixth day of June, the sun was still up. With the heatwave underway, the short walk to our vehicle was blistering agony. There was a patch of green growing between the cracks on the pavement. It could be the beginnings of the organic vegetation that we had long been hoping for. Or it could be something else—anything that might be expected from a newly unplugged world. There was not enough time, however, to inspect it in more detail. The priests convening by the doorway of the nearest chapel always appeared to be hungry—indeed, they were said to be at their hungriest at this time of the year. We rounded the curve until we could no longer see them.

That night, sitting in what remained of our living rooms, we watched the evening news play out an all-too familiar narrative: how a band of savages avoided detection and managed to slip in, ransack and loot 108 Tower at 9 Elone Street. There was no mention of the unplugged machine. The world, in its initial wave of overhaul, was already starting to forget that the machine had even existed.

The Outsiders

"So this is how it is outside the cage, huh?"

"That's not eagerness in your voice, is it?"

"I mean, just look at this. What happened to this place? It doesn't even look remotely like the one we saw on the projector."

"What do you mean by 'what happened'? Nothing happened to this place. Something happened to us. The projector had a 95-percent confidence level. What we're seeing now falls within the acceptable margin of error built into the system."

"I just didn't imagine it would be like this. After all we've been through—all those years of staying up late for the show, all those we had to betray to get hold of those rare passes, the amount of poison we had to ingest, the required number of kills just to get a slot for the audition—all for this, this stupid, miserable wasteland. We're so screwed. This is worse than dying, you know."

"Strange that you haven't realized it yet. We're already dead."

"Well, you could say that. You've always been keen on simplifying things."

"I simply call out what I see and—"

"Hey, do you see those? They—those things out there—they change. They look like ferns. And then horses, except they're not horses. And they're most definitely not ferns."

"I know. I've been watching them since we got here. I don't think they can hurt us though. We're past being hurt—physically, that is. If we get near them, those creatures are probably just going to ignore us. They'll just go about their lives, if what they do qualifies as life."

"Should we try and touch them? What do you think?"

"At this point, it doesn't matter what you and I think. Let's go."

"Where?"

"Does it really matter where we are going?"

Anno Domini

A familiar routine unfolds in and around the museum in the desert. It is a Tuesday, eleven years after the fireball of methane bubbles in the thawed Siberian permafrost.

Museum visitors who prefer a more circuitous route than the sleek walkway installed for their convenience enter the building by circum-navigating a construction site shielded from view by one-way Slip™ panels. They can hear the voice of the ailing Mr. Cash through that one-way shielding. In the concealed construction site, the ailing Mr. Cash is still calling out about something, something terribly important, something about how everyone he knows goes away in the end. As usual, many in this group of museum visitors cannot hear Mr. Cash over the noise of the power drill and the idle talk of Silent Ray, who will not shut up, cutting across the lull of the wasteland's sweltering desert heat. Meanwhile those museum visitors who are more conditioned by the lack of immediacy of the times with which they are made to thrive enter the building by taking the motorized guided walkway.

Both groups of museum visitors are directed into a spacious, well-lit, sparsely decorated lobby. A glass dome, a customized ISO class 1 cleanroom, squats low in the middle of that space. Inside the dome is Damien Hurtz, kept conscious yet immobile by drugs for twenty-nine years as of this count. Understandably, Hurtz has been propped up to mimic the pose of the shark he used for one of his art exhibits. It will not be long before yet another playful kid attempts to bash the unbreakable glass enclosure.

Directly beyond the full reconstruction of the Library of Alexandria and south of the vast museum interior is a lead-lined booth. Outside this booth is a man seated on an uncomfortable stool. His facial features are plain, forgettable. The same can be said for his real name. In the museum, he is nicknamed the Lone Operator, a moniker once intended as a slur. His job entails two things: accept a token coin and never refuse entry—not for any reason. The lead-lined booth is an assisted suicide chamber of sorts. The patron pays a token coin, enters the booth, selects from the menu of predestined places and times, then pulls the lever to get conveyed to that chosen time and place. All patrons know the drill. The knowledge is hard-coded within everyone, pretty much the same way spiders know instinctively how to spin webs. A three-minute window is available for anyone who wishes to change their mind. One can still safely return intact during this three-minute period, which is chimed every thirty seconds by a trusty cesium-133 clock. At the end of three minutes, the physical body disintegrates as it is no longer synced with the present. Nobody has ever come back alive, except for one woman in 2017. Interestingly, the top-selling place and time in the Lone Operator's booth is Wembley Stadium on July 12, 1986, a few paces in front of the stage where Freddie Mercury, wearing a yellow jacket, is doing improvised vocalizations before performing 'Under Pressure'.

Among these museum regulars is a spindly stranger—yet another spindly stranger scrutinizing Jürgan Temnaut's painting *The Bass Player in the Fifth Circle of Hell*. A much stranger-looking stranger walks among these museum regulars. He has a lesion on his upper left arm, a once-necrotic lesion exposing part of the bone and the ravages of flesh permanently marred by Krokodil. No one can see the manifold disfigurements in this man's body but it does not mean they are not there. This stranger-looking stranger is likely to join the people huddled in the corner where the candied head of the last emperor is displayed. Almost all the people in that part of the museum chuckle as they speak ill of the dead.

The regular museum hours are not complete without the spectacle of an elderly being wheeled before a Picasso, where he will cry out, either due to frustration or senility, variations of "What has changed since the last time we were here?" The museum also has to play host to an occasional child, molded in the same destructive behavior as his parents, staring with that telltale glaze-eyed gaze at the huge aquariums of the last surviving specimens of freshwater fish. This child will ask his mother, "Why do the fish move like that? Are they excited because they can see us?" His mother, molded in the same destructive behavior as her parents, will say, "No, that's because the fish have gone crazy. All sentient animals are driven insane by captivity." Delighted by the idea of inflicting suffering, mother and child will laugh just like the generation preceding them.

Outside the museum and out there in the world: the perpetual heatwave. In the nearby construction site shielded from view by one-way Slip™ panels, the voice of Mr. Cash is still drowned out by the noise of the power drill and the idle talk of Silent Ray, who will not shut up. The hammering and the yammering of mechanical jaws disturbing the earth cuts across the lull of the wasteland's sweltering desert heat. Inside the museum: the visitors, most of them damaged goods, remain past their expiration date and linger all cut up and irreparably broken. They have long been broken inside, and *inside* is where repair becomes close to impossible.

Eventide

It is not yet officially morning but everyone in the world has already reported waking up from dreams either completely coated or partially encrusted with black mold. The general consensus: it is black mold, all right. Even as people continue to worship their symbols in churches, where the misguided notion of the serpent as the primal usurper is perpetuated. Even as people avoid the streets and the great outdoors, where the heatwave stockpiles its projected daily death toll. The scourge of color in dreams has been identified as black mold through and through. It has been said that this black mold demonstrates no affinity to moisture so it does not appear glossy and is not wet to the touch. *Its surface is dry*, they say—but not out loud. It is as if there is tacit agreement among people—among all dreamers—that articulating this fact will make it harder, will make it impossible to purge. That it might make the black mold want to stay for good. Then nobody will dream in color anymore.

So this day's bulletin talks about how yellow peeks from underneath the blackness of the mold—as seen through the gauze of sleep and lucid dreaming. In its partial erasure, yellow is said to have become more vivid, more memorable even as it occurs in a dream. One dreamer talks about how raw egg yolk gets slowly obscured by a creeping film of mold. She says it appears as if during its eventual consumption by black, yellow asserts its polish, glows more brightly than usual in preparation for its obliteration. She insists that she has never seen yellow to be *that* beautiful before. Then there's the dream about a couple and the dream canaries, which the couple say are kept in a cage. And this dream couple, whose teeth are coated with fuzzy black mold, smile next to the caged canaries resplendent in yellow that looks more real than yellow can ever be outside of a dream. Another man talks about a dream where black mold has begun to take over a yellow lampshade. He says that the blackening has started at the base. He swears again and again that he has never seen yellow to be *that* beautiful before, right before the yellow lampshade is completely overtaken by black.

It is not yet officially evening but everyone in the world now dreads having to go back to sleep. No one is eager to know what dream color gets overtaken by the dream mold this time. It turns out that it is green. Green, as in the verdant green fields that have long ceased to exist in this world.

Green, as in the verdant green fields everybody forgets are not really vegetation at all. They just look that way to anyone searching for a way out of this wasteland. Green, as in the pulsing bottle-green-colored scum that blankets a shallow pond under the leaking wastewater tank. Green, as in the forest beyond the clearing, where a tourist guide sells maps and says, "Tell me where exactly in the trail you want to go, and I'll tell you what you are made of." The tourist guide manages a store, a store that is also a tiki hut with torches on each side. The torches blaze black fire as the black mold has already taken over all shades of yellow and their variations. Inside the store that is also a tiki hut, souvenir keychains and paperweights of scorpions and spiders encased in clear Lucite blocks are sold. Behind one of the glass shelves where merchandise is kept, there is a woman, possibly wronged in all ways that a woman can be wronged, who foams at the mouth. She spews crumbly black mold and spouts words not quite intelligible. Yet, everyone can hear her. "Meet me in the place of nightmares," she must have said at some point. And because this occurs in a dream and because nobody will ever dream in color again, there is no way to say no. And because nobody will ever dream in color anymore, everyone going through this same dream buys one of the keychains sold in the store that is also a tiki hut.

The paperweights of scorpions and spiders encased in clear Lucite blocks are too bulky, too expensive for most citizens in this dream world. Nobody buys the paperweights, just the keychains. The keychains are supposed to glow in the dark. But they can't glow anymore. Not when everything's coated with black mold, whose surface is said to be dry although no one is brave enough to say that out loud. Because nobody will ever dream in color again, someone out there might think of angling his newly bought key chain towards the dimming light, angle it in the hope that it might glow. And the key chain might still glow. He might still catch a glimpse of the faltering glow-in-the-dark green before the black mold, before the blackness finds a way to slip over and engulf everything.

Demolition Day

Dear Vasquez,

Vasquez, dear Vazquez, where were you that sixth day of June, when the bombs were dropped on 108 Tower at 9 Elone Street? For a moment there, I forgot that you died the day before June 6—that you missed the once-in-a-lifetime spectacle that the local television news station dubbed 'demolition day' by 26 hours.

Although I never liked you very much, especially the way you so blatantly kissed ass on your way to the top of the bureaucratic totem pole, I did not particularly relish the thought of you dying by choking on a portion of ham sandwich that you bought from the vending machine in the pantry. They said there was mayonnaise all over your clothes. Someone said "Creampie cum got him." Two people laughed. One was the maintenance guy sent by the vending machine company. They also said that, as you gasped for air, you made sounds like a grunting horse or a swine in heat. They made lewd jokes about you, Vasquez. Maybe it was because you reminded them of their own mortality, that they would someday die and die alone, die alone as just another inelegant bead added to the inelegant creampie-cum-got-him string. You reminded them of how easy it is for life to be snuffed out and how such a life was not all that special to begin with. Consider the finality involving a morsel of ham sandwich stuck in the throat. The water cooler bubbling next to your slumped form. Clerks and middlemen going about their business in the building. The centralized air conditioning's balm of salvation against the heatwave outside. The Lord of Song piped in by the FM radio speakers in the lobby. Phones rang, either answered or ignored. Extension lines lit up their cold translucent eyes of false immediacy. The entire world oblivious to the passing of what it deemed yet another expendable.

Dear Jordan,

Jordan, dear Jordan, where were you that sixth day of June, when the bombs were dropped on 108 Tower at 9 Elone Street? Were you still hung up on the phantoms of your past? I know, I know how you were supposedly made from scratch: coffee and sugary pastry, spontaneous generation and malingering, impulse and genuine wanting. But you were anchored somehow and whatever held you down seemed like a deadweight, one that was inescapable and permanent. During your formative years, you might have seen how your mother was beaten up by your father. How her spine remained taut against the broken glass on the floor. No restraining order could stop him. During your formative years, you might have also seen how your mother beat up your dog. How her tight grip on the broom handle made the veins on her hand stand out, stand out as taut as her lifelong greed for material things. You said you had forgotten how your parents died and when. It might have been during the house fire, the night of the storm, the crossfire at an intersection in Avenida. But you remembered how relieved you felt the day you learned of the news, didn't you? You could not tell whether or not there was blood on your hands. It just might be grease on them—that time. Or brake fluid. It was brake fluid, wasn't it? Although you would not admit it even to yourself, you did wish they had suffered in the end.

In grade school, you were this little pale, little freak, little needy bastard who could not lend us your ear. You selected your silences depending on how cornered you felt. There were times, too, when you could not stop yourself from approaching strangers to ask why on earth they had to keep wearing your face. They called you crazy every time you asked for your face back. Someone eventually punched you, cracked your incisor.

Jordan, Jordan, I saw you in some photographs. I work with a lot of photographs these days. I work for the State, so I cannot tell you what the deal is with these photographs. I saw you photographed in the background of two women posing next to plastic pine trees. In that photograph, you were checking out the stunted palm trees sold in a booth next to an ice cream truck. I also saw you photographed among the bystanders behind a cop mediating between two drivers who were skirmishing over a fender-bender. Then it was you again, in yet another photograph and so on and so forth—each time the camera's depth of field underscored the fact that you would remain for most of your life consigned to the periphery.

Dear Samael,

Samael, dear Samael, where were you that sixth day of June, when the bombs were dropped on 108 Tower at 9 Elone Street? Do you still remember me? Listen, you know me from childhood.

I work with a lot of photographs these days. I work for the State, so I cannot tell you what the deal is with these photographs. In one of them, a still from CCTV footage, I recognized you. You had just arrived at the airport terminal. You arrived too late. You were supposed to catch a red-eye flight, economy class as usual, but your plane had long since departed without you. The baggage carts were all stowed away next to the stainless steel bins. The harried flight attendants had already gone through the motions of faking their beautiful smile, of finishing the pre-takeoff demonstration of slipping on life vests or buckling seatbelts or using oxygen masks, even the requisite handing out of drinks to the finicky ones in business class.

The plane crashed. You took the train. Everywhere, the heatwave. But it did not bother you that much anymore.

Dear Gregson,

Gregson, dear Gregson, where were you that sixth day of June, when the bombs were dropped on 108 Tower at 9 Elone Street? Did you oversleep? Or did you once again choose to stay awake all night long—awake just staring at the ceiling, because you were having far too many nightmares lately? Were the nightmares about people being blown to bits after you looked in on them—with your drag-and-release sensor scoping and scanning degree by painful degree with crosshair-precision on the screen—deploying guided bomb units from miles away where it was safe and forever air-conditioned to counteract the heatwave outside? Tell me, tell me, Gregson, do you still see through grainy infrared when you dream? I'm pretty sure you do. There were no signal jammers for the images in your mind.

I met you once as a tenant in an apartment building where all the units were windowless. You

24

were the tenant obsessed with wanting a view—a view of the park where an algae-encrusted pond sat in its fits of stagnation, gleamed with its mouth full of green. But there were no windows in that apartment building. There were no windows in all the other apartment buildings in the city. There were no windows left in this world. It was just the heatwave, the well-insulated and air-conditioned structures, bombs being dropped like those used on 108 Tower at 9 Elone Street that sixth day of June.

I work with a lot of photographs these days. I work for the State, so I cannot tell you what the deal is with these photographs. I don't have a photograph of you, Gregson, but I know exactly what you see on your screen moments after you hit, where it says "INIT" on the payload console that you nicknamed Mama. There's a brief flash of light on the upper right-hand corner of your screen. That brief flash of light obliterates a dot superimposed on the upper right-hand corner, a dot that corresponds to someone once alive.

The Early Signs of Blight

When the bad man once again came to see ten-year-old Ben, the boy did the usual: screamed for his Mama. Ben told his mother that this time the bad man had managed to reach out from the confines of the closet, had reached out without fear of the yellow light of the Pooh lamp, had reached out with a blackened arm that was long enough to encroach into Ben's world, and had grasped the end of the bed sheet. At first, it was just an arm—impossibly long and snakelike, skin burned uniformly throughout its length. And where the burnt outer skin had peeled away, the flesh underneath revealed a fleshy pink tone, the color associated with healing.

Ben had expected the bad man to finally show himself. The rest of him, not just his arm. The bad ones always did. The bad always came out of the woodwork and showed themselves to the world. Ben had not expected that it would start its journey into his world with an arm alone. The arm, after grasping the cotton sheet, withdrew. It disappeared again inside the slightly opened closet

door, a testing of the waters of what Ben expected
to be its gradual trespassing into his world.

His mother, upon hearing the screams,
entered the room. She hugged him.

"He's back," Ben said.

"I know, I know, I know," she said, releasing
her son from her embrace and heading out of
the room again. She returned with a sponge and
a bucket of soapy water that smelled strongly
of bleach and cleaned the insides of the empty
closet. She would end up ruining the wood with
her forceful rubbing, but she did not care. She
wiped away the nonexistent blood with calculated
strokes, wiped away the origins of the beast, crying
as she did so but not noticing it until she felt spent
and tired, the acrid sting of bleach everywhere.

In the midst of his mother's manic cleaning,
Ben fell asleep, inhaling the bleach's fumes. He
snuggled into his pillow. The blanket covered his
body, except for the feet. He could not sleep with
his feet under the blanket.

There was Pooh on the lampshade casting a
warm amber glow, one that enlivened as much as
it concealed. There was Pooh on the lampshade,
and he was holding his pot of honey, his grin
locked in place.

The next morning, Ben came bounding out of his room and smiled at his mother as he met her worried gaze. She instantly brightened and motioned for him to join her at the breakfast table. She sipped coffee, looking outside the kitchen window of their two-bedroom apartment at Station Tower, the five-storied apartment building that had stood for close to one hundred years at the junction between Outerbridge and Bardenstan.

The whole apartment smelled faintly of bleach slowly dissipating out of one living room window that had been left partly open. It looked as if she had spent the entire night cleaning. The lopsided coffee table had been straightened, its edge lining up with the striated pattern of the area rug. The edge of the yellow ottoman was aligned squarely with that of the coffee table. The rug was fluffed and freshly vacuumed. Four throw pillows, all in varying shades of grey, were arranged according to size on the couch. The magazines on top of the coffee table were organized in stacks of two—the thick ones on the left, the thin ones on the right. The pile of thick magazines towered over the thin ones, and this unnerved Ben. He crossed the room and placed some of the thick magazines on top of the thin ones to balance the height of the piles. Satisfied, he went to the kitchen.

She poured milk and proffered the glass to her son. He took his accustomed place at their small dining table and drank without meeting her inquiring eyes. "I'm okay, Mama," he said, as if anticipating a question from her. He always made an effort to reassure her, even when there was no reason to. She smiled at her little boy, a smile she reserved for the people in her life whom she loved unquestionably.

It was the first Sunday of December. The cold was underway. In the distance, the Fletcher Memorial Home squatted, its silvery industrial-grade paneling glinting. In the streets below, there were only a couple and a woman walking her dog. Jim Shenkel, Station Tower's dayshift doorman, shuffled with his familiar gait by the side of the building, checking whether the vandals had spray-painted the walls again. Last week, someone had spray-painted GOD LIVES HERE in red.

"Are you crying again, Mama?" Ben called from the couch as he watched *The Land Before Time*. There was no way that he could tell she was crying because he could not see her face. She was hunched over the sink, scrubbing at the already spotless metal surface.

"No, honey," she said, steeling herself not to cry again.

That night, Ben covered himself with the blanket up to his chin and prayed the same memorized lines his mother had taught him to say each night—"as I lay me down to sleep". The prayer did not ward off the bad man. It certainly did not make him feel safe, even during the times when he recited it fervently. But he relied on his mother's instincts to survive, and if she believed that the verse about dying while asleep and being delivered straight to Heaven could save him, then he would gladly say it.

She was still fussing in the kitchen. The whole of the afternoon, she sorted the dried laundry from the downstairs laundry room and wiped the windows and the empty top shelves.

Ben saw her, or thought of seeing her in his mind's eye as she sought for more and more things to clean. His last thought before he drifted off to sleep was this: she should have been here, protecting him in case the bad man showed up again. He absently scratched at the healing cuts in his abdomen.

Hours later, Ben woke up, feeling a tug on his exposed left foot. He threw his blanket aside and looked down where the bad man's fingers grappled at him, pulling him into the gloom of the closet. Holding on to the metal headboard for balance, Ben screamed.

His mother entered the room, still clutching a dirty rag. When he looked at his foot again, the bad man's hand had disappeared. He could not remember how long his mother comforted him before he fell asleep. When he woke up, it was past six in the morning.

With a soft knock, his mother peeped through the gap of the slightly opened door and told him to get ready for breakfast. She made an omelette with cheese and some meat trimmings. She slid the egg onto his plate, then paused as she heard a knock.

Ben could only hear parts of their conversation. He did not pay much attention to them. There was no need to. He and his mother had more serious problems to contend with—a bad man in the closet and Ben's mother losing her job a week ago—than a stranger appearing at their doorstep on a Monday morning.

"I'm Officer Subic, Mrs. Bruin."

"What's this about?"

"Can we talk to you in the police station, ma'am?"

"Just tell me what this is about."

"Someone from your husband's office called us. He hasn't shown up for work for three days and his cellphone's been turned off. And when they called you, you said that he had already left you and your son."

"That's correct."

"May I come in, ma'am?"

"Sure."

They talked for a long time. Half an hour or more had passed before the door latch finally clicked into place.

Ben's mother once again busied herself with household chores. At Station Tower's apartment 11, there was never a shortage of surfaces and corners to dust, of table cloths and couch covers to straighten, of home decorations to wipe down and rearrange.

Meanwhile, Ben, inside his room, had advanced eleven breathtaking pages through his copy of Maurice Sendak's *Where the Wild Things Are*. The pages were filled mostly with illustrations. Ben sometimes touched the book's pages and imagined feeling the vibration from the pacing of the characters in the book.

That night, Ben woke up with another tug at his foot. This time, it was much more forceful. Without looking down, he knew. He understood that the manner in which the bad man had grasped his foot, the scrabbling nails digging deeply into his skin, the bad man's rot seeping in through those scratches, meant that the bad man would not let him go this time. He would end up another blackened, disfigured creature in the closet, known henceforth to the world as nothing more than a bare arm worming out of every bedroom closet door. He shrieked.

Predictably, Ben's mother entered the room and switched on the overhead light. Instead of the usual cleaning rag, this time she clutched a knife, swung it and slashed at the stunted form in the middle of the bed, the form that tormented and lived, tormented and loved, tormented and demanded, again and again, to be rescued.

"It's me, Ma," Ben said twice as he fended off the blows with his small hands.

"Leave us alone, leave us alone, leave us alone," she raged in a monotonous tone and, exorcising all the evils harbored by the flesh, slashed with her knife until the flailing stopped.

The police, toting the search warrant the erstwhile Officer Subic hadn't possessed the day before, broke down the door at ten minutes past seven in the morning.

They found Ramona Bruin rinsing dishes in the kitchen—dishes that were already clean. She looked out of the small kitchen window by the sink, a window the size of a submarine porthole showing the off-white of winter, the near monochrome universe that beckoned to no one because there was nobody else outside.

"It's over now," she said to the officer.

On the bed was Ben. Ben, who could not sleep with his feet under the blanket. Ben, who no longer stirred and was covered by the bedclothes up to his chin. On the bedside table, the Pooh lamp burned a striking yellow orange, the picturesque tinge of a summer afternoon sky created by air pollution and thermal inversion.

The officer who peeled away the covers made an effort not to retch. This was only his second homicide. In the closet, another officer found a mannequin's arm. Then someone remarked on the incredible cleanliness of the rest of the house, except for the blood Mrs. Bruin had tracked across the floor.

A day and a half later, Carlos Bruin's body—what was left of it—was discovered in a dumpster behind the Fletcher Memorial Home, a short walk from Station Tower. The head and pieces of his torso were stashed inside a wheeled trolley bag. The limbs were not located.

The shaken residents of Station Tower were interviewed by the police. Some were guarded in their responses. Some were open to speculating: everything from child abuse to how Ramona Bruin had been driven to insanity when she lost her job. Claire Dalkey, who owned a unit on the first floor and who had lost her son in an accident weeks ago in front of the building, said something about not bothering to find out what had happened to the Bruins because nobody could ever know the truth. "Perhaps, it was all random, and she just snapped," she said.

The news told of self-inflicted wounds on Carlos Bruin's abdomen. They were all superficial and in various stages of healing. A similar pattern of cuts was discovered on the boy's stomach.

Nobody could piece together exactly what had happened at Station Tower's apartment 11. Months later, in another part of the city, almost the same thing happened—mother and son, two-bedroom apartment, a mannequin's hand in the closet, self-inflicted wounds on the abdomen in different stages of healing when the son's body was found, and the mother near-catatonic and scrubbing a perfectly clean kitchen countertop. And once again, someone noted the orderliness of the apartment. It was as if everything was buffed and straightened out by mechanical hands. It was as if there was something underneath all these— the clinical neatness, the incredible attention to detail, the absence of family photographs, and the seemingly contrived cleanliness—that was yet to be uncovered. Even then, no one could figure out the whys.

The third time a similar yet still unsolved case landed on the precinct just outside the border of Outerbridge, one detective unwittingly intuited the truth. "When we impose so much order onto our lives, it upsets the balance, you know, the natural chaos of things. Then it explodes back in our faces. Then we just kind of—snap."

"Trying to channel your inner Carl Sagan, Jess?" said Brenda from internal affairs, holding a measuring cup full of coffee grounds in the pantry.

Everyone laughed, but the laughter was born out of nervousness and frustration. It was going to be a long day.

The Neighbors

Suarez, understandably losing track of dates and times, woke up sometime midmorning of November 24. The clanging and banging supposedly produced by his next-door neighbors startled him. The loudest of the sounds was distinctive: metal lids striking their pots with festive urgency. As if preparations for a feast were underway. There was the faint scrunch of stainless steel knives against cruciferous vegetables on wooden chopping boards. Then the quick shuffling of feet, the sliding of chair legs across linoleum floor, the ping of an oven bell. Suarez willed himself to close his eyes long enough, focusing only on the sounds. Only then was he able to forget—temporarily of course—that there was nobody out there to produce such a racket.

In the stuffy darkness of his bunker, he stretched his arms and legs, felt the familiar pitch and yaw of boredom, an unshakeable deadweight. Long gone was the spellbinding sway of strange machines, their consoles backlit by yellow light. The pilot lights, which helped him control the various aspects of his underground home, used to fascinate him. But at the end of the first year, Suarez found himself covering them with opaque pieces of woven fabric, hiding their reassuring glow that indicated normal levels of temperature, humidity and breathable air drawn from aboveground and passed through a series of filters.

At last the recorded sounds ended, leaving him with the grating spokes in the wheel of routine: the remote shifting of the solar panel assembly, the jerry-rigged telescopic array that enabled him to observe the outdoors—what was left of it. And there it was again, the scarecrow he once mistook for a man. It still looked artificial, symmetrical, humanoid: a disruption in the long-gone green fields beyond. All had turned gray now, the color of estrangement, stability, and out-of-sync spectral drift in the ceramic grating that lined the underside of the flooring beneath his feet.

Tomorrow, although it was too soon for Suarez to hope since he had set his plethora of 916 digital morning waking sounds to randomly shuffle, he might wake up hearing the hush of country winds and the cock-a-doodle-do of a faraway rooster announcing the break of dawn. Or it could be a suite of nature sounds that called to mind a land of fog and decade-old trees, leaky log cabins and small houses, their chimneys spewing smoke, their interiors buzzing with the collective drone of chunky turntables and 1980s rock 'n' roll. All iterations of audio effects that called forth the groan of a civilization that had grossly miscalculated its goals for immortality, whispering over and over, stifled at times yet always unrelenting, whispering over and over *not alone, not alone, not alone.*

The Longest Night

For the third time, Ellen Machin asked for permission to turn on the light. She said she could no longer stand the dark. Before that, she had complained about a lot of things—her prickly blanket, her two-day-old canker sore, and Poochi, the family dog, burying his head in her pillow no matter how many times Ellen shooed him away. But Jack knew that his five-year-old daughter's tantrums boiled down to one thing: *the dark.*

"Just a spark, Daddy," she pleaded.

"Keep your hands away from the switch, young lady," he said. He only called her "young lady" when he was irritated.

Like other middle-class families, the Machins conserved energy and only resorted to their meager light sources when necessary. The last time they had decided to use the lone five-watt overhead lighting fixture was three days ago. That was when they needed to adjust the thermostat to the lowest bearable temperature setting and to strategically position their foodstuffs and utensils so they could easily eat in the dark. They had to make the energy last to provide heat for their small underground basement and for the occasional cooking.

As much as possible, Jack Machin insisted on bundling several layers of thick wool blankets to counteract the cold.

It was the eighty-second day of the longest night. Every 42 years, the planet was blanketed in darkness for nineteen months and three days.

"What do we do tomorrow, Dad?" Ellen asked

"We sleep, honey. We sleep. Then we wait for morning."

The mention of *morning* was not meant to comfort Ellen because they knew it would remain dark. But it felt good to say the word once in a while. Besides, conjuring the image of sunrise would not hurt. Sunrise would spell hope, would dispel the foreboding of a long season of rambling what-ifs. What if the planet's elliptical orbit stretches further, expanding its circumference and lengthening the nineteen-month darkness? This had been observed in a similar-sized planet in NGC 1300. What if nobody survives through to the sunrise? What if everyone succumbs to loneliness or to the eventual bouts of depression brought about by hormonal imbalance? What then?

When they sat down in the dark, they usually talked about the bouts of vivid dreams. Jack and

Anita took turns explaining to their daughter that the strange dreams resulted from the long period of uninterrupted darkness. It increased the rate of melatonin production in the pineal gland, leading to vivid dreams. Anita said that she had dreamt in sequence, and she was confident she could sustain the sequence. For four days, she had the same dream: preparations for the annual town fiesta. In the dream, she was making ensaladang pako, fish balls, and pancit bihon. Jack was able to control the timing of his dreams, too. In his dream, he was learning martial arts. He enjoyed that dream and had it "programmed" to replay the same scene in which he finally earned a brown belt. The only thing he willed to change was the intensity and duration of the applause from his dream-audience.

The Machin family had just eaten MY San's Sky Flakes biscuits and sardines in olive oil. They ate in the dark and scraped the bottom of the tin cans with their forks. Poochi slurped his meal from his doggie bowl.

Anita had run out of ways to entertain her family. She played the guitar in the dark yesterday. Ellen sang along with her mother. Jack, who pretended to like the tune and was grateful for the darkness that concealed his reaction, appreciated his wife's doggedness to keep the family up and about. For two hours each day, he switched on the small transistor radio. The government broadcasts always ended on the same note: an emphasis on exercising and staving off the eventual depression that came with this long period of darkness.

A siren wailed outside. It was probably another suicide. Jack told another joke, which made Ellen laugh.

Boltzmann Brain

We hope you are out there, and that you are reading this message. We are broadcasting from 78°14'09"N 15°29'29"E, the Svalbard Global Seed Vault. On this day 70 years ago, the planet's last polar bear Arturo died, his body freed at last after 22 years of slowly going insane from the sweltering heat and unremitting stress of captivity in a concrete pit at Argentina's Mendoza Zoological Park. On this day 85 years ago, collared, chained, drugged and used as a mascot for the torch ceremony of the second to last Olympic Games, one of the last remaining jaguars in the world was gunned down when it attempted to escape from the clutches of people wanting to take selfies with it. On this day 92 years ago, the last remaining species of *Ceratotherium simum cottoni*, the magnificent northern white rhinoceros, was killed by a poacher who bribed one of the guards in a nature reserve in Sudan. And on this day 150 years ago, we were like you in many ways—either well-dressed in a corporate office in one of the world's megacities or hunched in capitalist enclaves toiling to earn our hourly wage—kidding ourselves again and again that the human race was worthy of celebration.

We are now preparing the deployment of a robotic feeler in the Phrumsengla nature park in Bhutan. Thick smoke has been spotted by an aerial go by courtesy of a newly repaired Hover-567. The smoke may be from a human encampment. We hope that this mission will yield something, someone. Numerous bees and butterflies have been sighted in and around Phrumsengla. Pollination activity is proceeding as expected for a protracted summer.

Meanwhile, one of the lateral heat-sensing screens shows a walrus and its calves two miles from here. They seem to be frolicking in the snow. They can laze all they want in this infinity of cool reflective whiteness. Nobody will ever hurt them again.

It is still relatively dark outside the vault. It is always relatively dark.

We hope you are out there, and that you are reading this message. We are broadcasting from 78°14'09"N 15°29'29"E, the Svalbard Global Seed Vault. On this day 61 years ago, the Amazon carbon sink failed. It failed permanently. The primeval rainforest, which once drew atmospheric carbon for storage in its soil or trees, was emitting more greenhouse gases than it could take in. On this day 102 years ago, it was discovered too late that all the plastic waste dumped in what was formerly known as the United Kingdom were being washed into the Arctic region within two years. Autopsy results showed that all the marine animals collected in that region for the next one hundred years had plastic inside them. And on this day 98 years ago, the melting of the permafrost in Siberia was finally kicked off by years and years of massive deforestation. Subterranean craters were revealed once the trees that had insulated the frozen ground for millions of years were removed. With these craters came the release of methane into the atmosphere, effectively accelerating global warming.

Then the eventual megaslump, the precession of the Earth's axis from the melting of the Antarctic and Greenland ice sheets, the dominos that mark all possible paths to extinction quietly falling in place. Then came the isolated tribe in Peru, driven from their native land by a four-day wildfire. Four days in the city square, and they started succumbing to various illnesses as they had neither developed immunity nor been vaccinated against even the most ordinary diseases. One even contracted a common cold and ended coughing up lung tissue, throat swollen and bloodied, until he died. All in all, 16 out of the 89 members of the Peruvian indigenous tribe survived.

Remember how it all started in the once frozen north. Remember the thawing of the permafrost that bared all—the anthrax outbreak in Russia and then the mutation and subsequent spread of the once dormant 50,000-year-old *Mollivirus sibericum* virus, first discovered in the vicinity of Chukotka in East Siberia, the subsequent deaths of women. Patient Zero was Dr. Emilia Gattskill of the Global Climate Research Center. Survivors of the deadly disease, who were mostly men, were ultimately felled by extreme weather disturbances and the drought from the eternal summer in the few yet-to-be submerged habitable parts of the world.

Right now, we take a look inside the twentieth floor of an apartment building submerged 18 stories down. Inside a living room, there is a framed poster of a wind turbine whose nacelle and rotor blades are on fire. Atop the turbine are two men, their sole exit blocked by the roaring fire. They are embracing, waiting for the flames to engulf them. Black mold has taken over this living room, the bedroom, everything.

On days like these, we wish we could pat a domestic dog for comfort. We wish we had conventional hands to pat a domestic dog. But a body with conventional hands—the human body—is a ruinous construct, prone to injury and susceptible to the ravages of time.

Are you out there reading this?

We hope you are out there, and that you are reading this message. We are broadcasting from 78°14'09"N 15°29'29"E, the Svalbard Global Seed Vault. On this day 119 years ago, the Syrian civil war saw the bloody takeover of Aleppo. On this day 143 years ago, Heinrich Himmler bit into a cyanide pill one day before his scheduled interrogation for war crimes. And on this day 123 years ago, over 1,000 members of the Glorious Dawn cult, hastening their journey to a promised utopia, committed mass suicide by drinking cyanide-laced purple Kool-Aid.

On the slopes of Mt. Chimborazo in Ecuador, we maintain a base camp. Thankfully, it is still fully operational after all this time. A long time ago, it was built for a geo-engineering project that aimed to regulate the earth's climate through the aerial spraying of aerosol. The aerosol droplets were believed to reduce ground solar radiation. By then, the project was already too late to make any difference to the rising global temperature.

The base camp has just sent its weekly readouts. As usual, atmospheric and ground readings are consistent with the projections of the Copenhagen Diagnosis. Microscopic extremophiles, the only signs of life, teem on the surface of the rocks.

Are you still out there? Let us know.

We hope you are out there, and that you are reading this message. We are broadcasting from 78°14'09"N 15°29'29"E, the Svalbard Global Seed Vault. On this day 286 years ago, Iqbal Masih was born. Iqbal Masih was a bonded child laborer in Pakistan. When he was ten years old, he escaped from the carpet factory, where he had to work in order to pay off his family's loan. Then he helped release more than 3,000 children from illegal slavery in Pakistan before he was murdered at age twelve. On this day 187 years ago, South Korea at last, although a century too late to spare millions of dogs, put an end to its Boknal dog meat festival. Spain followed but not soon enough, putting an end to its Toro de la Vega bullfighting event. And on this day 154 years ago, five firemen put out the fires in a nuclear reactor in Chernobyl. They knew that no protective suit in the world could shield them from the radiation around the reactor. They died painful deaths within 36 hours of exiting the power plant, successful in preventing the catastrophic effects of the meltdown.

Today, a manually controlled probe has parachuted and safely touched down at Tristan de Cunha. We remotely guided it to check the houses for human survivors. None. This far-flung place in the southern Atlantic Ocean once had a maximum total population of 272 people. Tomorrow—still on schedule—we'll make a sweep of the Huascarán National Park in Peru. We hope to find you there. If not, we will try again. Next stop is the Tanggula Mountains of Tibet.

Hope, hope is a good thing. We hope to see you soon.